The Fabled Stables

TROUBLE WITH TATTLE-TAILS

BY

JONATHAN AUXIER

ILLUSTRATED BY

OLGA DEMIDOVA

AMULET BOOKS · NEW YORK

Library of Congress Control Number for the hardcover edition: 2021005270

Paperback ISBN 978-1-4197-4273-6

Text © 2021 Jonathan Auxier
Illustrations © 2021 Olga Demidova
Book design by Heather Kelly

Printed and bound in China
10 9 8 7 6 5 4 3 2

Amulet Books are available at special discounts when purchased in quantity for premiums and promotions as well as fundraising or educational use. Special editions can also be created to specification. For details, contact specialsales@abramsbooks.com or the address below.

Amulet Books® is a registered trademark of Harry N. Abrams, Inc.

ABRAMS The Art of Books
195 Broadway, New York, NY 10007
abramsbooks.com

Rude spirits of the seething outer strife,

Unmeet to read her pure and simple spright,

Deem, if you list, such hours a waste of life,

Empty of all delight!

—Lewis Carroll

1

AT THE TOP OF THE WORLD SAT AN ISLAND.

At the heart of that island lived a boy named Auggie.

Auggie was just like most other boys, except in one way. He had a *job*.

Auggie worked in the Fabled Stables—a magical place full of one-of-a-kind creatures.

Usually Auggie loved his job. But not today. Today he had a problem.

Auggie was taking care of the Unfeeling Brute.

This was a tricky task, because Auggie had no idea what the Unfeeling Brute wanted from life. The creature had no eyes, no ears, no mouth, and no nose. Auggie was *pretty sure* it had a head, but he couldn't be certain.

Willa the Wisp drifted over. "Any luck?"

Auggie sighed. "Only bad luck."

Auggie flopped to the ground. "I've tried singing to her, feeding her, and taking her for a walk . . . but she won't respond."

"Maybe she wants to tickle fight?" Willa was always up for a good tickle fight.

Auggie picked up Fen and waved him in front of the Brute. "Maybe she wants to play fetch?"

Fen wriggled out of his grip. "*Maybe* the thing just wants to be left alone. *Some of us* like being left alone."

This was a rude thing to say, but what do you expect from a *literal* Stick-in-the-Mud?

2

AT THAT VERY MOMENT, IN A VILLAGE FAR AWAY,

a bell was *ding-ding-ding*ing as loud as loud could be.

It was an alarm bell.

It belonged to a bank.

A bank with an open front door.

Two thieves strolled through the halls. They wore dark cloaks with heavy hoods. They had loot sacks and lockpicks. They had plans and schemes.

There was a vault in the basement of the bank. A vault with a one-of-a-kind treasure. The thieves

walked into the vault and swiftly swept the treasure into their bags.

And why didn't the guards stop them?

That is a very good question.

3

AUGGIE WAS ON THE ROOF, cleaning out the Bizzybee hives.

He was still thinking about the Unfeeling Brute. "How do you help someone who doesn't want anything?"

Willa was trying to catch a Bizzybee in her paws. "Maybe Fen is right," she said. "Maybe we should just leave her alone?"

"OF COURSE I'M RIGHT!" Fen called from inside a hive.

Auggie wiped the beeswax off his hands. "I'm not ready to give up just yet."

When Auggie came to the island, he made a promise to care for all the beasts in the Fabled Stables—even the hard-to-love beasts. He didn't stop caring for the Bizzybees just because they might sting him. "Whatever the Brute needs, it's my job to help."

"I know!" Willa said. "We can ask Professor Cake what to do!"

Professor Cake was the man who owned the island. He was very old and very clever. He was also very busy.

"I know I shouldn't bother the Professor," said Auggie, "but maybe just this once—"

WORK-SHOP

BOOM!

Suddenly, the stables SHOOK and SHUDDERED and TWITCHED and SPUTTERED.

A moment later, everything was still again.

Auggie picked himself up. He and Willa looked at each other.

"A new arrival!" they cried.

4

SOMETIMES THE FABLED STABLES CHANGED TO MAKE
room for a new beast. The whole place would
rearrange itself, and then Auggie would find an
empty stall that led to a beast somewhere in the Wide
World. It was Auggie's job to go out and rescue that
beast from danger.

"Race you there!" Auggie shouted.

"I win!" Willa cried from two floors below.

"I'll get you next time," Auggie said, catching his breath. He slid down a rope and landed beside her.

A new stall had appeared right next to the Unfeeling Brute.

Auggie looked at the words on the sign:

"*Tattle-Tail*?" Willa wrinkled her nose. "That doesn't sound like a very friendly thing."

Auggie rolled up his sleeves. "Friendly or not, it's our job to help."

"What did you say?" Fen knocked the side of his
head. "I think I've got beeswax in my ears!"

"You have ears?" Willa said.

Auggie paced in front of the gate, thinking.
"First we'll need supplies. We can't march in
unprepared."

"You can't march in *underwear*?" Fen repeated.
Sort of.

Auggie looked at the world beyond. Who knew what dangers could be waiting for them? "We'll need a lantern, and some rope, and a bag, and a map, and my field book, and . . ."

Willa skip-hopped over the gate. "Last one there's a rotten egg!"

"WAIT!" Auggie called.

But she was already gone.

Auggie grabbed hold of Fen. "It looks like a Stick-in-the-Mud is all the *supplies* I'm going to get." He hoped it would be enough.

"Away I go."

And away he went.

5

AUGGIE FOUND HIMSELF IN THE MIDDLE OF

a village. A sign over the gate read "Welcome to

Rainbow's End."

The streets were empty. The stoops were empty.

The shops were empty.

Auggie shivered. "The whole place looks abandoned."

"*A Band-Aid*?" Fen picked wax from his ear.

"Are you hurt?"

Willa's tail twitched tall.

"There's someone hiding close by

. . . I can *feel* it." Willa could always

tell when people were playing hide-

and-go-seek. "Come out, come out,

wherever you are!"

"Over here!" A voice squawked.

"In the alley!"

Auggie saw a lady peeking out from

the corner. She looked nervous. She

looked tired.

"Oh, hello," the lady said, with a weak smile.

"I, um . . . didn't see you there."

A furry face appeared next to hers. "That's a lie,"

the face said. "She was spying on you."

The woman shuffled out from her hiding spot. "It's true. I was afraid you were more robbers." She offered her hand. "I'm Mayor Clover."

The furry face leaned over her shoulder and said, "I wouldn't shake that hand if I were you. Right before you got here, she was picking her nose."

"I was not!" Mayor Clover said.

"Check her finger if you don't believe me."

Auggie peered at the talking creature. It was fluffy. It was long. It was shaped exactly like a *tail*. "My name is Auggie, and I'm looking for a one-of-a-kind creature called a Tattle-Tail."

Mayor Clover sighed. "Well, you've found it. Only it's not one-of-a-kind anymore." She raised her voice. "You can all come out now!"

Dozens of other people shuffled out from their hiding places.

Every one of them had a tail!

WILLA CLAPPED HER PAWS. "This isn't a rescue . . . this is a *party!*"

Auggie wasn't so sure. Every person in town looked miserable. "How did this happen?" he asked.

And so Mayor Clover shared her *tail of woe . . .* "It all started when I found a box in the courtyard. The box wasn't addressed to me, but I was curious. I pried open the lid . . .

"To my surprise, the box was empty! But when I turned around, I discovered that this strange creature had attached itself to me. At first, I thought I might enjoy having a tail. But then I learned something else about the tail . . . it could *talk*!

She opened the box! It wasn't addressed to her, but she opened it anyway.

"Every time I did something even a little bit wrong, the tail made sure everyone knew about it.

"I wasn't the only one in trouble. My tail seemed to be able to multiply. Soon every person in the village had a tail of their own.

"The tails created so much confusion that when the robbers showed up, no one was there to stop them!" Mayor Clover shook her head. "And we've been stuck with these things ever since."

MAYOR CLOVER LED THEM TO A TOWER at the end of

the square. "This is where it all started," she said.

Auggie heard a *ding-ding-ding*ing sound coming

from inside the tower. "Is that an alarm bell?"

"What's an *alarm smell*?" Fen asked.

Mayor Clover explained, "Rainbow's End is home to a legendary pot of gold. If you take a coin out of it, two more appear inside. We keep it safe inside our bank. Two guards protect it day and night—"

"Not anymore!" said another Tattle-Tail.

Two guards in uniforms shook their heads. They had tails, too.

"It's our fault," the first guard said. "We were so busy arguing with each other that the robbers walked right past us. And now we've lost our precious pot!"

"Precious *snot*?" Fen said. "Gross."

Auggie knew he wouldn't get much done if Fen kept interrupting. "I'm worried about that wax in your ears," he said. "Why don't you go clean up?"

Fen gave him a confused look. "If you say so." He shrugged and wandered off.

Auggie turned back to the mayor. "I can't help you catch the robbers, but I can help these Tattle-Tails."

"Yep!" Willa gave a proud pirouette. "It's our job to save one-of-a-kind creatures from danger!"

"But they're not in danger," the mayor said. "We're the ones in trouble."

Auggie didn't want to argue. "In either case, the first step is to get them off you." He looked at the shops around him. What could he use to lure away the Tattle-Tails?

And then he got an idea . . . a tempting, tasty idea!

8

AUGGIE BURST FROM THE BAKERY with a tray full of bagels and brownies and cookies and cakes. "Come big, come small, come snacks for all!"

The tails looked at the food. They opened their mouths. And they . . . tattled.

You'd better hide that cheesecake. It makes the mayor gassy.
Keep Horace away! He already ate two breakfasts!

Ophelia just double-dipped!

Before Auggie knew it, arguments had broken out all across the village. "Apparently Tattle-Tails don't care about food," he said.

Auggie and Willa tried everything they could think of to safely remove the Tattle-Tails.

They tried SCARING them off!

TICKLING them off!

TEARING them off!

And TRICKING them off!

But nothing worked!

"It's hopeless," Auggie said, flopping to the ground.

"Ow!" a voice belted from below. "He's trying to smoosh me!"

Auggie jumped back up.

His eyes went as wide as cherry pies.

A new Tattle-Tail had appeared . . . and it was attached to *him*.

9

WHILE AUGGIE WAS GETTING USED TO HIS NEW TAIL, Fen was wandering the streets of Rainbow's End, more than a little confused.

Auggie had told him to "go clean up," but that was *not* what Fen had heard.

"'*Gold* clean up,'" he muttered. "What does that even mean?"

That's when he noticed something on the street.

It was small.

It was round.

It was *gold*.

"Now I get it!" Fen picked up the

piece of gold and threw it in a trash can.

He found another piece of gold nearby. And then

another. And another.

"I'm doing an excellent job!" he said to no one in particular as he threw more gold into the trash. "People could trip over these!"

Fen followed the trail of gold coins all through the village. "I wonder who dropped all this gold."

He soon found his answer, when—

AAH!

FEN STARED AT THE ROBBERS, who were huddled in an empty schoolhouse. They had dark cloaks with strange marks on the front. These weren't just robbers . . . these were *ROOKS*!

The Rooks were a secret group of villains. They were always trying to steal one-of-a-kind things for their own wicked ends. They had once tried to capture Willa. And now they had stolen the pot of gold!

"Help!" Fen screamed. "It's the Rooks!"

The first Rook raised a fistful of sparkling dust. "Zip it!" she said. "Or I'll *curse* you with PIXIE POWDER!"

The second Rook raised a pair of scissors. "And I'll snip you to bits with these MAGIC SHEARS."

Fen was about to be frightened, but then he noticed something. "Hey," he said. "You've both got tails!"

The first Rook's tail said, "For the record, that's not really pixie powder . . . it's *glitter*."

"And those are just craft scissors," said the other tail. "They can barely cut paper."

Fen scowled at the Rooks. "Why are you both hiding in here? Shouldn't you be long gone?"

The first Rook rubbed her temples. "The Tattle-Tails were supposed to be a distraction, so that we could rob the bank. But before we could escape, we caught tails of our own. We had to hide in here so no one would hear them blabbing."

"We've been here all night," the other Rook said. "Every time we try to sneak outside, they start calling for help." He looked like he was about to cry. "I just want to go home."

"You just want a *goat poem*?" Fen was having trouble following all this. "Whatever. I'm getting out of here."

The Rooks stepped in front of him. "If you leave, you might tell people where we're hiding." They folded their arms. "You're not getting out of here without a fight."

Fen couldn't hear what they said, but he had a pretty good idea what they meant. "Have it your way!"

Fen, you will remember, was a Stick-in-the-Mud. He could shift shape into any manner of useful tools.

He stretched out his branches and started to change into something large, something heavy, something *hammery*.

11

BACK IN THE VILLAGE SQUARE, Auggie was losing

hope. He had tried everything he could think of to

help the Tattle-Tails . . . but nothing had worked.

"What's Professor Cake gonna say if I fail?"

Auggie's tail piped up. "Everybody, look! Auggie's

about to cry."

"I am NOT," Auggie said, blinking.

Willa tried chasing her new tail but tripped and crashed. "Ugh. Two tails make me all *wobbly!*"

Auggie stood up. "There must be some way out of this." He looked around the square. What could he use to get the Tattle-Tails back into their crate?

Auggie heard a *clink clink clink* at the end of the street. He turned and saw Fen carrying an enormous pot of gold.

"You found it!" Mayor Clover called. "Rainbow's End is saved!"

Fen had no idea what she was saying. "I cleaned up all the gold, lady!" he said.

"What about the *robbers*?" Auggie made sure to speak clearly so Fen could understand him.

"I cleaned them up, too . . . if you know what I mean." Fen explained how the Rooks had tried to hold him prisoner. But he had managed to knock them out cold. "As soon as the Rooks went beddy-bye, their tails just wandered off."

Sure enough, two Tattle-Tails were slithering down the street. Auggie watched as they slinked right past him and curled up inside the open crate. "It looks like they have no use for sleeping people."

"That's it!" Mayor Clover snapped her fingers. "We can use that talking stick to knock everyone unconscious."

"Wait!" Auggie looked from Fen to the crate. "Everyone in town got a Tattle-Tail . . . except Fen."

Willa gave Fen a cuddle. "They must have sensed his inner goodness!"

"More like his inner boringness," one of the tails called from inside the crate.

"Yeah," the other groaned. "He can't hear a word we say."

"Is that true?" Auggie turned back to Fen. "They left you alone because you couldn't hear them?"

"Beats me." Fen mined a gob of wax from his ear and flicked it on the ground.

Auggie looked at Fen's wax-covered branches.

And that's when he got an idea . . . a buzzy, brilliant idea!

12

AUGGIE MADE EVERYONE LINE UP IN FRONT OF FEN.

He scooped out chunks of wax from Fen's branches
and handed them out.

"Ignore your tails, and just
mind your beeswax!" Auggie called.
"Put it firmly in your ears."

His own tail muttered something about how that was disgusting. But Auggie couldn't hear. He was too busy minding his beeswax.

"No pushing. No cutting in line," Willa said. "There's plenty for everyone!"

There really was plenty. It was amazing how much beeswax Fen had in his ears.

One by one, the villagers put the wax in their ears.

And one by one, the Tattle-Tails got bored.

Auggie's own tail flopped to the ground. "It's
working!" he shouted. He watched as his tail slinked
across the square and back into the waiting crate.

"Bye-bye!" Willa said as her tail wriggled away.

As the last tail disappeared into the crate, Mayor Clover shouted, "Good riddance!" The whole town let out a cheer!

Auggie approached the open crate. When he got there, he saw that all the other tails had vanished. Now there was only the first one. "That wasn't so hard," Auggie said.

"Tell that to them," the tail muttered, peering over Auggie's shoulder.

Auggie turned around to see a very angry crowd moving toward him. Mayor Clover shouted, "Quick, before it escapes! Lock that crate and throw it in the lake!"

Auggie blocked their way. "No locks," he said. "That's not how we treat wild beasts. It's my job to care for all creatures—no matter how hard-to-love."

Auggie had never talked to a grown-up like that.
He hoped it wasn't too rude.

Mayor Clover looked at him for a long moment.
"You've got one minute to get that thing out of my
town." She pointed to the clock. "Otherwise, you're
all going into the lake!"

Auggie needed to get the Tattle-Tail to safety—and fast! But he knew some beasts couldn't be rushed. He turned back to the tail. "What's your name?" he asked.

The tail scowled up at him. "Nunya."

Auggie spoke in his gentlest voice. The voice he used on his crankiest critters. "Hello, Nunya. My name is Auggie, and these are my friends Willa and Fen."

"Best friends!" Willa cried.

"*Not* your friend," Fen said. "We've been through this."

Auggie said, "We've come to bring you to the Fabled Stables—a safe place without crates or robbers or anyone who can bother you."

"Also lots and lots of beeswax," Fen said. "So don't get any ideas."

"You have to promise not to multiply again," Auggie said. "We only have room for you."

"No tattling?" Nunya scowled. "You can't just stick me in some stable and expect me to be happy. If I don't have someone to tattle on . . . I'm nothing."

Auggie thought about this. He knew the creature was right. But who in the stables would agree to having a Tattle-Tail?

And that's when he got an idea . . . an inscrutable, insensible idea!

13

"CAREFUL nOW," AUGGIE SAID. "You don't want to startle her."

"As if we'd know," Fen said.

Auggie gently placed the Tattle-Tail on what he *hoped* was the backside of the Unfeeling Brute. He stepped back.

"Well?" Willa said. "How does it feel?"

Nunya the Tattle-Tail blinked his eyes. "Hmm . . ."
Suddenly his fur puffed up. "I . . . I can feel what
she's thinking."

Auggie smiled. He had hoped this would solve
more than one problem. "Can you tell if the Brute
wants anything?"

"Let me check." Nunya cocked his head to one side
like he was listening. "She wants . . . a window so she
can feel the breeze."

"A window!" Willa cheered.

Auggie clapped his hands. "One window coming up!"

"Hang on," Nunya said, "she's just getting started."

she also wants a blanket at night!

And a warm oatmeal bath! And a pet rock!

And two pairs of shoes! And a theme song! And a balloon!

And one of those little hamster-wheel things, but bigger!

And a cool nickname! And something she calls "elephant pants"!

And dancing lessons! And . . .

The Tattle-Tail told every little wish and secret that the Unfeeling Brute carried inside. It was a long list, and at some point Auggie lost track.

"Looks like these two are a perfect match," Auggie said.

"Perfectly *irritating*," Fen groaned.

Auggie nudged the Stick-in-the-Mud. "You saved an entire village *and* stopped the Rooks. For someone who claims not to care about helping anyone, you sure are good at helping everyone."

Fen squinted and wiped his cheek. "Excuse me," he muttered. "I must have beeswax in my eye."

AT THE TOP OF THE WORLD SAT AN ISLAND.

At the heart of that island lived a boy named Auggie.

He cared for beasts of all kinds.

Some were strange.

Some were dangerous.

Some were hard-to-love.

But every one of them belonged.

WHAT ONE-OF-A-KIND CREATURE
WILL AUGGIE MEET NEXT?

FIND OUT IN THIS SNEAK PEEK
OF BOOK 3!

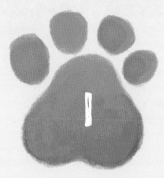

AT THE TOP OF THE WORLD SAT AN ISLAND.

And at the heart of that island lived a boy named Auggie.

Auggie wasn't the only one who lived on the island. There were his friends, Willa and Fen. There were the beasts that he took care of at the Fabled Stables. There was the mysterious Professor Cake, who owned the island. And there was Miss Bundt, the groundskeeper.

This was Auggie's home, and he loved every inch of it.

Today, Auggie was helping Miss Bundt at the Paradocks. Professor Cake had asked her to build a boat.

"Is the Professor going on a trip?" Auggie said.

"The Professor never leaves the island." Miss Bundt unfurled a patchwork sail. "Besides, I don't think he'd fit!"

Auggie picked up Fen and started to swab the deck. He thought about who might fit in a boat this small. "Easy with the suds, kid," Fen said. "Bubbles give me the burps."

Auggie felt his ears go red. "My name is not *kid*." He hated when Fen called him that.

Fen rolled his eyes. "Who cares?"

"I do!" Auggie stopped swabbing. "In all this time I've been on the island, you have never *once* said my name."

"What's your point?" Fen changed himself back into a regular Stick-in-the-Mud. "Look, kid, when you've been at the Fabled Stables as long as I have, you learn not to bother with names. People come and go. There's no point in getting attached."

He turned and hopped back to shore, leaving Auggie behind.

2

THAT NIGHT, AUGGIE HAD A TUMMYACHE. He couldn't

sleep. All he could think of were Fen's words:

People come and go.

There's no point in getting attached.

Auggie's time on the island had been the happiest

of his life. He had friends. He had a home. He had a

job at the stables. But what if it wasn't forever?

He knew there had been caretakers before him. He hadn't thought about why or how they left the island.

Did they fail at their jobs?

Did the Professor send them away?

Auggie worked very hard to care for all the beasts in the Fabled Stables. But what if that wasn't enough?

He thought of the little boat floating in the water— ready to carry someone off the island.

What if that boat was meant for him?

3

THE MORNING WAS ALMOST OVER when Auggie
dragged himself out of bed.

"Look who decided to join us," Fen said.

"Sorry." Auggie wiped crust from his eyes. "I was
up all night, thinking about leaving the island."

Fen gave him a funny look and then shrugged.
"Like I care."

Hungry beasts

SNORTED and STOMPED

and SNUFFED in their

stalls—Auggie was late with their breakfast.

Auggie sang like he always did: "Come big, come

small, come breakfast for all!" He reached for his

Horn of Plenty, which . . . wasn't there. "Oh no!

I must have left it back in the treehouse."

"I'll get it!" Willa said and zipped off.

Fen hopped clear of a hungry snark. "You better hope

Sparklebutt finds that Horn before the beasts revolt."

BOOM!!!

The stables SHOOK and SHUDDERED all around them. The floor opened up beneath Auggie's feet—

"Whaaaaa!"

He tumbled two

stories and landed

with a SPLASH!

"I found the Horn of Plenty!" Willa floated down next to Auggie and helped him to his feet. "I didn't know the stables had a pond."

"They do now." Auggie wrung out his shirttails. "I think it's for a new arrival."

Auggie loved new arrivals—it meant another one-of-a-kind beast to care for. He looked up at the sign that had appeared above the stall.

He read the name slowly. "'Shib-bo-leth'?"

"What a silly name!" Willa said.

Auggie turned back to the stall. "Silly or not, that creature needs our help."

A swirling portal appeared above the water—somewhere on the other side was the Shibboleth.

"I can't see anything through that fog," Auggie said. "Where do you think it leads?"

ABOUT THE AUTHOR

JONATHAN AUXIER is the *New York Times* bestselling and critically acclaimed author of *Peter Nimble and His Fantastic Eyes*, *The Night Gardener*, *Sophie Quire and the Last Storyguard*, and *Sweep*. He lives with his family in Pittsburgh, Pennsylvania. You can find him online at thescop.com.

ABOUT THE ILLUSTRATOR

OLGA DEMIDOVA studied at the Moscow Art Institute of Applied Arts. Olga started work as an animator, but her tremendous passion for illustration changed the direction of her work. Now she works with publishers from all over the world to illustrate books and apps, mostly for children.